clown

farmer

lobster fishermonsters

doctor

salesmonster

librarian

street sweeper

captain

yeoman

photographer

golfer

television camera-monster

automobile mechanic

Little Monster®

Home, School and Work Book

By Mercer Mayer

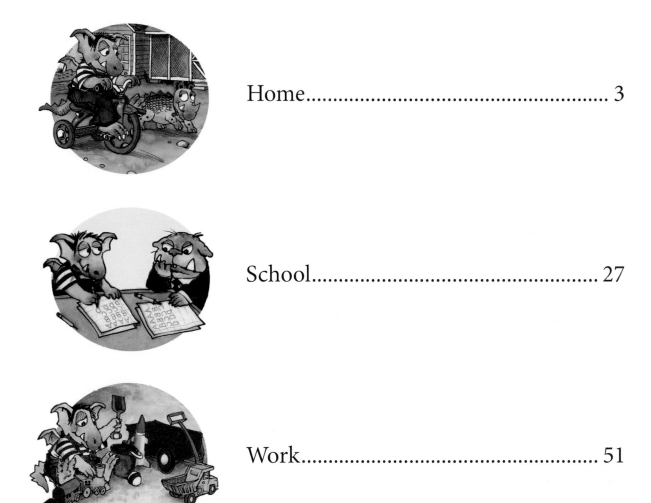

LITTLE MONSTER HOME, SCHOOL AND WORK BOOK
Copyright © 2012 Mercer Mayer
All rights reserved.

LITTLE MONSTER is a registered trademark of Orchard House Licensing Company.
All rights reserved.

Originally published in a different format by Western Publishing Company, Inc.
www.littlecritter.com

LITTLE MONSTER AT HOME
Text and illustrations copyright © 1978 by Mercer Mayer.

LITTLE MONSTER AT SCHOOL
Text and illustrations copyright © 1978 by Mercer Mayer.

LITTLE MONSTER AT WORK
Text and illustrations copyright © 1978 by Mercer Mayer.

Printed in China
46945201 2014

Published by FastPencil PREMIERE
307 Orchard City Drive, Suite 210, Campbell CA 95008
Premiere.FastPencil.com

Mercer Mayer's
Little Monster®

At Home

This is my house where I live with Mom and Pop. First there is my sister and then there is me and last of all there is the baby, who can't talk yet.

In the very bottom of my house is the cellar.
It's full of machines that make hot water and heat.

6

And in the very top of my house is the attic. It's full of great things that nobody uses anymore but we keep just in case.

My house is full of rooms. The kitchen is
for cooking and snacks.
I'm very neat and clean up sometimes.

In the pantry are all sorts of
cans and boxes and jars of food.
My mom makes the best apple jelly.

10

The living room is where we do things together. Pop reads his favorite book and Mom practices the violin. I bet I have the only mom in town who practices the violin.

Sometimes my sister and I play checkers. She usually wins. My pet Kerploppus sleeps on the couch, even though he is not supposed to.

12

When I have friends over, we go to the playroom. That way Mom isn't always telling us to be quiet. We watch TV and play games. The playroom is mainly for noise, and if you don't like noise, you'd better stay with Mom and Pop. They don't like noise either.

We have a workshop in the
garage. Pop is making a little
Croonie house. I am painting a
stool for Mom.

The laundry room is where my clothes
go when they get dirty.

And the bathroom is where
I go when I get dirty.

This is my room. It's full of
all my very own stuff. No one is
allowed in here except Mom and
Pop and my pet Kerploppus,
and my best friend. Not even my
sister, but sometimes I lend her
my baseball bat.

20

In the spring at my house, we take down the storm windows and put up screens to keep out the bugs. We plant our vegetable garden and beat the rugs. Everyone helps except my Kerploppus. He just gets in the way.

We throw away old stuff we don't want anymore. I always find lots of things I want to save, but Mom won't let me.

GARBAGE MONSTER PLEASE PICK UP

In the summer, we work in the yard. Pop prunes the apple tree, Mom cuts the grass, my sister trims the hedge, and I weed the garden.

In the fall, we pick apples for Mom's apple jelly. We get a pumpkin from the garden for a jack-o'-lantern. Pop works on the house and Mom rakes the leaves. I jump into the piles.

In the winter, it's too cold to stay outside for long, but at Christmastime Grandma and Grandpa come and we all go out and cut down our Christmas tree.

I like my house best in the wintertime because
when we get inside it's so very snuggly and warm.

Mercer Mayer's
Little Monster®

At School

Early in the morning, Mom
wakes me and says, "Get up,
Little Monster, it's time for
school."

I put on my overalls and go downstairs to breakfast.
Pop says, "What will you have this morning,

 or with ?"

lunchbox

crayons

pencils

notebook

apple for the teacher

After breakfast, I brush my teeth and get ready to go. I have lots of school stuff to carry with me.

Mom walks me to school.
Some of my friends come on a bus.

The first thing we do is sing a morning song and then we practice our letters. Yally makes some of his letters backwards and then be gets mad. But I help him.

Counting comes next. We count from one to twenty. Little Laff is the best counter in the class and that makes Yally mad, too. Yally wants to be the best counter in the class.

We have pets to take care of.
I have a Zipperump-a-zoo. Little Laff
has a gerbil. Grendella has a snake.
Yally won't take care of a pet. He
says they're icky.

We grow plants. Everyone is growing something different. I'm growing some beans in a box. Yally's plant won't grow. He says the plant is mad at him.

We tell what we did over the weekend.
Yally makes up the most fantastic stories.

On nice days, lunchtime is outside.
I have a sandwich and a tango, but Yally
always brings lots of candy.

At recess, we all go to the playground.
Yally won't play with anyone. He says games are stupid.

Hey, Yally, do you want to play ball?

After recess, Mr. Grithix reads us the story of Little Monster and the Three People. Everyone sits on a mat and listens except Yally, who pouts. He wants to hear a story about horrible people from outer space.

Mr. Grithix gets out a map and shows us where our town is. We see how the monsters dress in different countries, and look at flags from different monster lands.

We have science class and learn about leaves and rocks and bugs.

Then we get to make things. I make a
paper airplane, Little Laff makes a block
building, and Grendella makes a puppet.

Yally draws a great picture and everyone is amazed, especially Yally. Grendella says to Yally, "Yally, you're the best drawer in school." And Yally smiles.

Then we have singing.
Ms. Verakisser plays the piano.
Yally and I share a songbook,
and Yally even sings.

School is over. I walk home with my older sister and my new friend Yally.

I put Yally's great drawing on my refrigerator, right next to my great drawings.

Mercer Mayer's
Little Monster®

At Work

Places To Work

One day, Little Monster said, "Grandpa, Grandpa, what will I be when I grow up?"

"Come with me," said Grandpa,
"and we'll find out."

TINY CROONIES
ARE FUN

First, Little Monster helped build a road.

Next, Little Monster tried a job working with cars.

59

news anchormonsters

VERY BAD

The GREEDY GOURMET

MONSTER AT THE MOVIES

LATE NEWS

EARLY NEWS

camera 3

camera 4

news desk

studio electrician

klieg light

rain

snow

sun

cold

hot

100% LOW ACCURATE

38°

HI

72°

300°

-4

Then he became a TV star.

sponsor

floor speaker

THE RAIN WILL BE WET

YESTERDAY'S WEATHER TODAY

TROLLUSK BROTH... 3-RING

Hey, Grandpa, lookit me.

tightrope walkers
and riders

trapeze
artists

program
vendor

juggler

trapeze

tent
pole

bareback
rider

At the circus, Little Monster's
clown act was a smash hit.

With the story of his clown act on the front page, Little Monster thought he might try the newspaper business.

65

It was time for Little Monster's check-up, so he and Grandpa went straight to the Monsterville Medical Center.

67

But he came back
to Earth for lunch.

74

After lunch, they
watched Little Monster's
Pop building a house.

At the airport, Little Monster
visited the control tower.

79

"Maybe I'll be a scientist and study something," said Little Monster.

It just so happened that the great
Crafts Fair was going on that day.
"I love to make things, Grandpa,"
said Little Monster. "Let's take a look."

basket weaver

hand press

printer

brayer

rug maker

dye vat

dyer

bellows

forge

blacksmith

anvil

loom

weaver

yarn

knitter

87

It was time for dinner so Grandpa and Little Monster headed for home.

The next day...

businessmonster

dentist

pilot

glassblower

sculptor

pet

race car drivers

carpenter

weaver

figure
skater

policemonster

astronaut

camp
counselor

referee

hot dog
vendor

monsterologist